My Friend John

CHARLOTTE ZOLOTOW

illustrated by AMANDA HARVEY

A DOUBLEDAY BOOK FOR YOUNG READERS

A Doubleday Book for Young Readers
Published by
Random House Children's Books
a division of Random House, Inc.
1540 Broadway
New York, New York 10036
Doubleday and the anchor with dolphin colophon
are registered trademarks of Random House, Inc.
Text copyright © 2000 by Charlotte Zolotow
Illustrations copyright © 2000 by Amanda Harvey

Visit us on the Web! www.randomhouse.com/kids
Educators and librarians, for a variety of teaching tools, visit us at
www.randomhouse.com/teachers

Library of Congress Cataloging-in-Publication Data
Zolotow, Charlotte.
    My friend John / by Charlotte Zolotow; illustrated by Amanda Harvey.
        p.   cm.
    Summary: John's best friend tells everything he knows about John, the
secrets they share, their likes and dislikes, and the fun they have as friends.
    ISBN 0-385-32651-3
    [1. Best friends—Fiction. 2. Friendship—Fiction.] I. Harvey, Amanda,
ill. II. Title.
PZ7.Z77My   2000
[E]—dc21   98-54582
                                                                      CIP
                                                                       AC

The text of this book is set in 33-point Aunt Mildred.
Book design by Debora Smith
Manufactured in the United States of America
May 2000
10 9 8 7 6 5 4 3 2 1

For Ursula Nordstrom and Mary Griffith, with love
C.Z.

For Jonathan, Grace, and Jonah
A.H.

I know everything about John

and he knows everything about me.

We know where the secret places are

in each other's house,

and that my mother cooks better

but his father tells funnier jokes.

He can't spell

and I can't multiply
so we help each other.

His mother won't let him out if the weather's bad
but I can come over in any weather,

even if it's pouring rain or windy
or a blizzard.

We always stick together

because I'm good at fights,

but John's the only one besides my family

who knows I sleep with my light on at night.

He can jump from the high diving board

but I know he's afraid of cats.

I know what things he keeps
in his bureau drawers

and he knows what's in all the closets
at my house.

He saw me cry once

and the day he broke his arm
I ran home and got his mother for him.

We know what's in each other's refrigerator,

which steps creak on each other's stairs,

and how to get into each other's house

if the door is locked.

I know who he really likes

and he knows about Mary too.

John is my best friend

and I'm his

and everything important
about each other we like.